This book
belongs to:

....

This edition published in Great Britain in MMXVII
by Scribblers, an imprint of
The Salariya Book Company Ltd
25 Marlborough Place,
Brighton BN1 1UB
www.salariya.com

Text & illustrations © Yang Dong MMXVII
© The Salariya Book Company Ltd MMXVII

HB ISBN-13: 978-1-912006-60-1

1 3 5 7 9 8 6 4 2

A CIP catalogue record for this book is
available from the British Library.

Printed and bound in China

Printed on paper from sustainable sources

Visit
www.salariya.com
for our online catalogue and
free fun stuff.

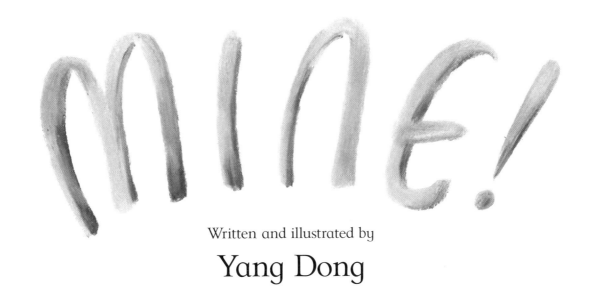

MINE!

Written and illustrated by

Yang Dong

SCRIBBLERS

a SALARIYA *imprint*

This year I got a rabbit for my birthday.
I love her so much!

I take her with me wherever I go.

I bake for her to make sure she eats well.

I run with her to keep her fit,
and give her a bath every day.

I dress her up in the latest fashions,

and I show her to my friends.

If I were a rabbit like her,
I think I would be very happy.

One night I dreamed that I was the pet, and my rabbit had to look after me.

She hugged me…

She fed me…

She took me running…

She washed me…

And she took me to meet
all of her friends.

I woke up feeling a bit frightened.

And I realised…

I didn't know her very well at all.

From now on, I will take extra good care of her.

I will respect her and make her feel safe.

I will find out what she really needs…

and what she really likes.

Because she is not just a pet...

She is my best friend.